Kate Leake

Who Ate The Cake?

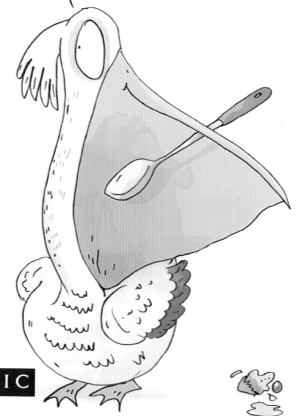

Bob was Freddie's dog.
He was always getting into trouble,
mostly for eating things that he shouldn't.

Freddie was Bob's boy.
Freddie was often in trouble, too, mostly
because he liked collecting things.

Every week, Freddie counted up his pocket money, and bought lots of new things from his Collectors' Weekly catalog.

So far, he had collected:

15 Toy cars

11 Comics

7 Cacti

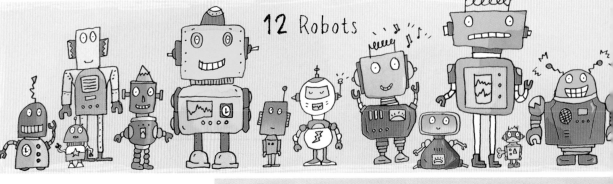
12 Robots

9 Trains

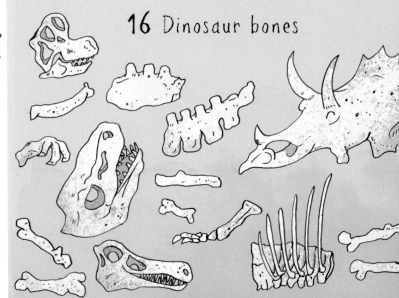
16 Dinosaur bones

5 Ships in bottles

10 Shark teeth

8 Cuckoo clocks

CUCKOO!

6 Snow globes

4 Pink ponies
(which he sent back)

3 Aliens

and a handful of creepy crawlies.

Bob loved Freddie's collection. It gave him plenty of interesting things to chew – especially the dinosaur bones.

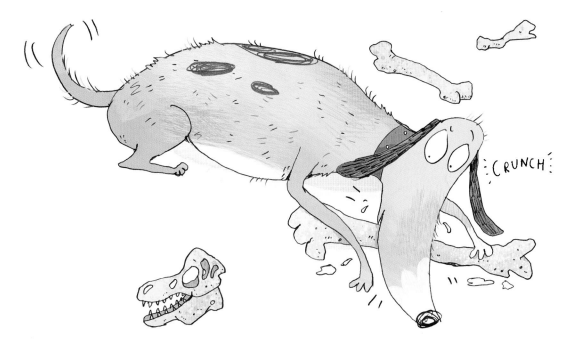

CRUNCH

Mom and Dad were less happy.
"Freddie!" they said. "There must be

NO more
things!"

But, that very afternoon, another huge box arrived. Freddie had ordered so many things from his **Collectors' Weekly** catalog, that he'd earned a mystery free gift!

Bob sniffed the box suspiciously. It smelled sort of . . . FISHY!

"We'd better not tell Mom and Dad about this," said Freddie. Then he lifted the lid and out popped . . .

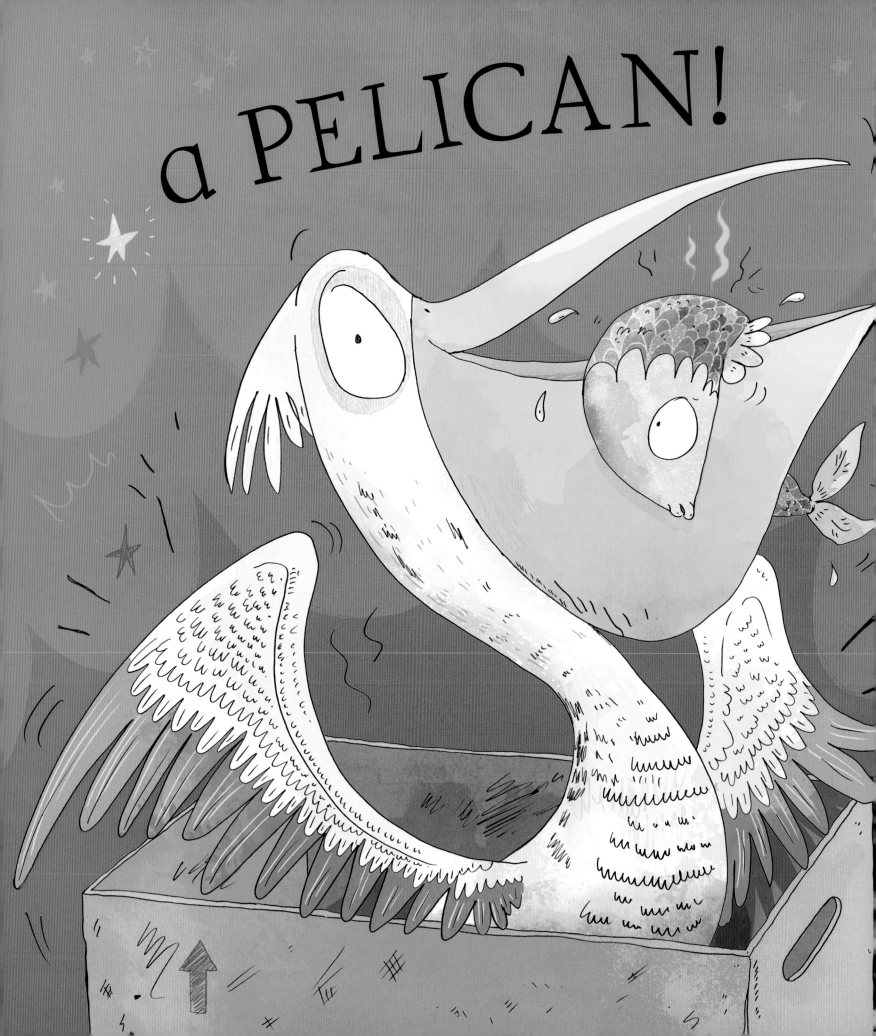

Freddie was **thrilled.**

But Bob didn't like the pelican.

It was **big.**

It was **flappy.**

SQUAWK!

And its beak was wide enough
to gulp down a computer.

HELP!

GULP!

Which is exactly what it did,
when Freddie wasn't looking.

"**No!**" barked Bob.

"Pesky pelican!"

"Shh!" said Freddie. "Mom and Dad mustn't find out about him!"

And that was just the start of the chaos.

First, Mom's knitting went missing.

"Grrr!" growled Bob. "Pesky pelican!"

Then it was Dad's daffodils.
"Huh?!" gasped Bob. "Pesky pelican!"

DAFFODILS

Then it was Grannie's best tea set (plus some very fine pastries from Paris.)

"Help!" said Bob. "Pesky pelican!"

Then it was ALL of Bob's favorite chewy toys.

"Nooo!" cried Bob.

Pesky pelican!

But did the pesky pelican get the blame? Of course not.
Nobody knew about *him*. They all blamed Bob instead.

"My knitting!" cried Mom.
"Bad Bob! No biscuit!"

"My daffodils!" groaned Dad.
"Bad Bob! No biscuit!"

"My tea set!" squeaked Grannie.
"Bad Bob! No biscuit!"

"My chewy toys!"
howled Bob. "Sad Bob!
More biscuits!"

But nobody understood him.

Bob decided that Pesky Pelican
was nothing but

big bad
beaky
trouble!

But the next day was Freddie's birthday. Bob was
determined to be on his best Bob behavior.
That way, he might get a piece of
Freddie's Big Birthday Cake.

The cake had been baking
all morning, and it smelled
SCRUMPTIOUS!

Bob tiptoed into the kitchen to have
another good sniff before teatime.

RAWR!

But he was too late!

With one big, beaky GULP, the pelican
ATE THE WHOLE CAKE!
There was nothing left but one
teeny tiny cherry ...

"Noooo!!!"
howled Bob.

"PESKY
PELICAN!!!"

He chased that pesky pelican all around the kitchen
– but the pelican was too fast and flappy for him.

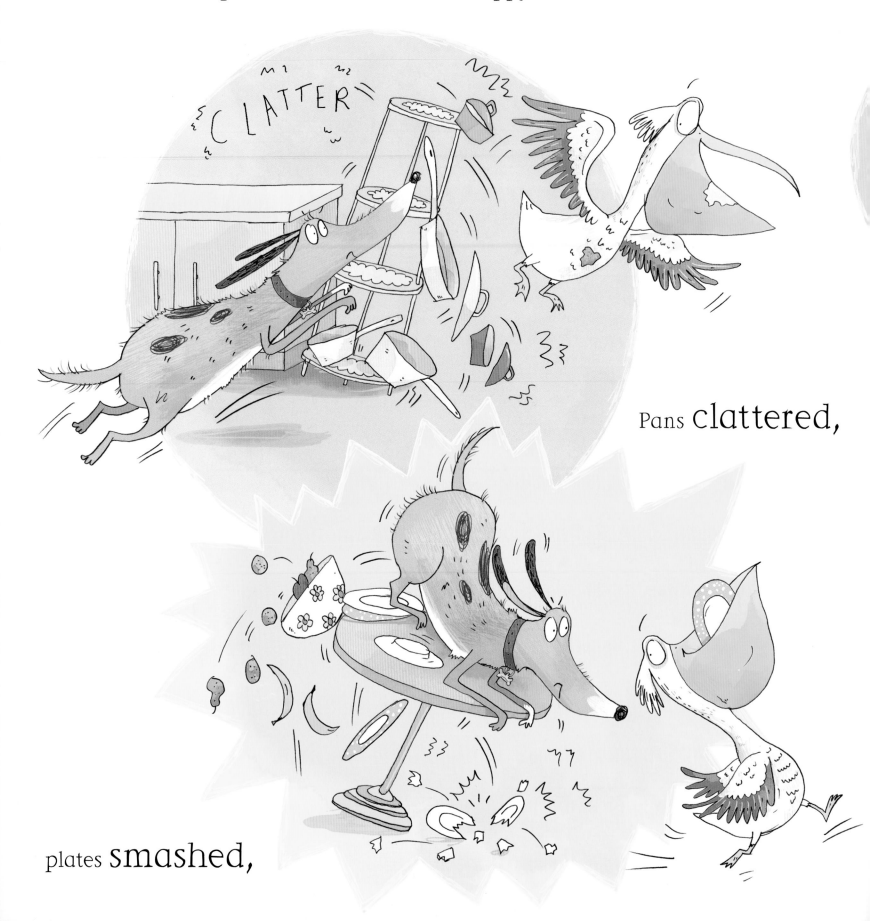

Pans clattered,

plates smashed,

spoons **scattered,**

food **splashed . . .**

. . . and everyone came running to see what the commotion was.

"My kitchen!" shrieked Mom.

"My cake!" said Freddie.

"Bad Bob!" shouted everyone.

"Look at this mess!"

There was custard on the windows, plates on the floor, jam on the ceiling, and a pelican on the fridge.

It took a long time to unpack the pelican's beak.
Inside, they found:

One entire Big Birthday Cake,
(minus one teeny tiny cherry),

Grannie's tea set

and some very soggy
pastries from Paris,

Dad's daffodils,

something that had
once been Mom's
knitting,

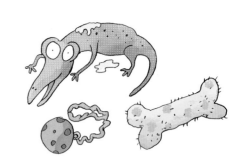

all of Bob's
chewy toys . . .

. . . and a whole lot of other
things they hadn't even noticed
were missing!

"Poor Bob!" cried everyone.

All those days of "No biscuit!"
and he'd not been a Bad Bob at all!
"Bob needs a treat!" said Dad. "What
would you like for tea, Bob?"

barked Bob.

And, for once, everyone understood him perfectly.

Bob ate a lot of sausages,

while Mom and Dad
stuffed that peckish pelican's
beak full of juicy fish,

help!

and Grannie and Freddie
baked another cake.

After all the fuss, it had turned into Freddie's
best birthday ever – especially when
there was a knock at the door . . .

. . . and another mystery
gift arrived!

First published in the UK in 2017 by
Alison Green Books
An imprint of Scholastic Children's Books
Euston House, 24 Eversholt Street
London NW1 1DB
A division of Scholastic Ltd
www.scholastic.co.uk
London – New York – Toronto – Sydney – Auckland
Mexico City – New Delhi – Hong Kong

ISBN: 978 1 4071 8067 0

For my WONDERFUL Alan,
with all my love xxx